A TALE FROM RUSSIA

THE BUN

MARCIA BROWN

HARCOURT BRACE JOVANOVICH, INC., NEW YORK

For Nadia

Library of Congress Catalog Card Number: 75-167832

ISBN 0-15-213450-6

Printed in the United States of America

First edition

B C D E F G H I J

Once there was an old man and an old woman.

One day the old man asked, "Old dear, will you make me a bun?"

"How can I do that? There is no flour."
"Oh come, my dear, scrape the bottom of the kneading-trough, sweep the bottom of the bin. Maybe we'll have enough flour."

The old woman took a hen's wing,
scraped out the bottom of the trough,
swept out the bottom of the flour bin,
and gathered together
two handfuls of flour.

She mixed the dough with sour cream,
shaped it into a nice round bun,
browned it in butter,
and set the bun at the window to cool.

The bun lay there very still,
until, all at once, he began to roll—
off the windowsill to the bench,
from the bench to the floor,
over the doorsill to the entry,

then plop-plop down the steps into the yard,
out through the gate, and
off and away into the wide world.

The bun rolled along the road until
he met a hare.
    "Little Bun, Little Bun, now I'm going
to eat you up!"

"Don't eat me, Little Hare,
and I'll sing you a song," said
the bun, and he sang:

>"I was scraped from the trough,
>I was swept from the bin,
>I was kneaded with cream,
>I was browned in a pan.
>By the window I cooled
>And had them both fooled.
>I dodged the old woman
>And fled the old man,
>And I can run away from you,
>Little Hare,
>That I can!"

And away he rolled, before the hare
could leap up to get a look.

The bun rolled on until he met a wolf.
"My Little Bun, I'll have to eat you up!"
"Don't eat me, Wolf! I'll sing you a song:

"I was scraped from the trough,
I was swept from the bin,
I was kneaded with cream,
I was browned in a pan.
By the window I cooled;
Now three are fooled.
I dodged the old woman,
I fled the old man,
I bypassed the hare,
And I can run away from you, Wolf,
That I can!"

And off and away he rolled before the wolf
could spin around to look.

The bun rolled on until he met a bear.
"A bun! A bun! I've been longing for one!
Now I'm going to eat you up!"

"How do you think you are going to do that,
old Heavy Head?

"I was scraped from the trough,
I was swept from the bin,
I was kneaded with cream,
I was browned in a pan.
By the window I cooled;
Now four are fooled.
I dodged the old woman,
I fled the old man,
I bypassed the hare,
I slipped from the wolf—
And I can run away from you, Brown Bear,
That I can!"

And away he rolled while the bear was
still rubbing his eyes.

On and on he rolled until up the road
strolled a fox.
"Good day. What a fine little bun you are!"

The bun began to sing:

"I was scraped from the trough,
   I was swept from the bin,
   I was kneaded with cream,
   I was browned in a pan.
   By the window I cooled;
   Five are now fooled!
   I dodged the old woman,
   I fled the old man,
   I bypassed the hare,
   I slipped from the wolf,
   Brown Bear couldn't stop me,
   And neither can you!
   Too bad, Fox!"

"Delightful song," said the fox, "but look here, Little Bun, I'm getting old and I don't hear very well. Sit for a while on my nose and sing that song again, but louder, please."

The bun hopped onto the fox's nose and sang his song once more.

"Ah, thank you, Little Bun! That is a charming song. If I could only hear it one last time.... Look, sit here on my tongue and sing it just once more."

The bun by now was quite beside himself. Like a fool he hopped onto the fox's tongue and—

Snap!   That was that!